Afterdark

The Afterdark Princess

ST NICHOLAS HOUSE
ABBOT'S HILL JUNIOR SCHOOL
BUNKERS LANE
HEMEL HEMPSTEAD
HERTFORDSHIRE HP3 8RP

Also by Annie Dalton

The next two books in the Afterdark series

The Dream Snatcher

The Midnight Museum

Night Maze

Out of the Ordinary

Naming the Dark

For younger readers

Space Baby

Tilly Beany

Tilly Beany and the Best Friend Machine

Tilly Beany Saves the World

Tyler Rapido Adventures

Tyler and the Talk Stalk

Dozy Rosy

The Frog Files

Jam Jar Genie

For Asha, Cherrie, Chia, Sebastian, Fleur and Joe

Contents

Chapter One
The perfect babysitter

Alice Fazackerly was the perfect babysitter. Anxious parents had only to set eyes on her to know Alice would never let them down.

Alice Fazackerly was not the kind of girl to give anyone a nasty surprise. She was as sensible as brown bread and butter. Her skirts were never too short. Her heels were never too high. Her skin was fresher than a summer daisy and she had a sprinkle of gold freckles across her nose. Her eyes were a clear sensible grey and her hair (which she never dyed purple), hung all the way down her back in one thick, sensible plait of shining chestnut brown.

Everyone said Alice was the best baby-sitter Forest Street ever had. And she was so obliging. No one ever had to rush out to fetch Alice before they'd properly finished drying their hair, because, rain or shine, Alice arrived on the dot on her bottle-green bicycle, which she propped against the garden wall and locked with a strong chain (wound around twice), before she rang the doorbell.

And whenever she came to babysit, Alice always carried her large leather school-bag slung over her shoulder, making it perfectly clear that once she'd settled the children with a bedtime story, she intended to work hard for her exams and would never allow *anyone* to stay up watching TV however dramatically they sulked.

Sometimes Alice gave the impression she could cope better than the parents themselves.

As for the children of Forest Street, they worshipped Alice. They couldn't wait for her to come again. It was quite a mystery to the parents. Alice was a nice enough girl, but not the least *bit* exciting.

Nor could the Forest Street parents understand why there was always such a terrible fuss if they changed their minds at the last

moment and decided not to go out after all. Scowls and howls. Tears and tantrums. Murder and mayhem.

'But you've absolutely *got* to go, Alice is coming!'

In fact children in Forest Street frequently reminded their parents they hadn't been to the cinema for weeks.

So Alice Fazackerly was always in demand and she babysat for every child in Forest Street except two. They were Kevin Kitchener (whose big brothers and sisters were supposed to look after him) and Joe Quail.

Joe Quail didn't have a brother or a sister, or a father any more and Joe's mum didn't trust anyone but herself to look after Joe in case he was taken ill or had a nightmare while she was out.

Joe was quite often ill and he had nightmares almost every night. Kit and Maisy Robinson heard him shouting through the wall. The Robinson family lived in the terraced house next door and, as it happened, Joe's mum worked at the same office as Mr Robinson.

Mr and Mrs Robinson went out more than any other parents in the street. They went to evening classes. They went to dinner with friends. They went to the theatre and the cinema. And sometimes they just went out dancing.

Joe didn't like the Robinsons. Their dad's beard was too black and bristly. Their mum laughed too much and she sang, loudly and out of tune, when she was hanging out the washing. Their mum was messy too. Once she went to fetch Kit and Maisy from school with flour on her nose from making a pie and Kit and Maisy weren't even embarrassed!

Whenever Joe heard the Robinsons laughing, an angry fist clenched in his chest, because he knew the Robinsons were laughing at *him* behind his back. Whatever Kit and Maisy did, Joe knew they did just to spite him. When Kit and Maisy let their rabbit out of its hutch, it headed straight into Joe's garden and ate Joe's mum's dwarf tulips before they even had a chance to flower. But when Kit and Maisy planted sunflowers, they grew so tall and flaunting they blazed right over the wall into Joe's garden, so they could spy on him, as he mooched about by himself.

Joe thought Kit and Maisy were loud, rough and raggedy and much too much above themselves, just like their rough, raggedy sunflowers.

Kit and Maisy never thought about Joe

Quail at all, if they could help it. They thought he was too boring for words.

But one windy autumn evening Alice Fazackerly rang the bell at Kit and Maisy Robinson's house and their mum sighed with relief, shutting the door just quickly enough to stop the leaves from blowing into the hall (but not fast enough to prevent Zoom, the stripy cat, zooming in under everyone's feet and tripping them up).

'Thank goodness you're here, Alice,' said Laura Robinson. 'We've got a problem. If Joe's mum can't find a babysitter she won't be able to go to the dinner dance with us and she hasn't been out to enjoy herself for so long. Would you mind if Joe stayed the night with Kit and Maisy? Oh-oh. Here come the outlaws!'

Kit and Maisy came roaring downstairs like twin hurricanes. Kit was a dark-haired hurricane with its socks hanging off the ends of its toes and the kind of face that made you think of a glowing holly bush, if you liked it, and trouble, if you didn't. Maisy's hurricane was dark marmalade and brown with streaks of silver. The marmalade was hair of the fleecy, frizzy uncombable kind. The brown was huge shining hazel eyes but also a baggy, knitted dress like a sack with moth-holes in it. The silver was old Christmas tinsel from the dressing-up box.

Alice took off her duffle coat, hung it neatly on the hook in the hall and ignored Kit and Maisy, who were nudging one another and pointing at Alice's leather bag, which was so lovingly polished that no one who didn't already know they were there, would ever have noticed the peculiar scorch marks on the front.

'Don't worry,' she said calmly. 'That's fine. Joe can come. No problem.'

'Oh,' moaned Maisy. 'Joe Quail is so-o boring. He's as boring as a beetle. He's a misery boots. He's a grumble-guts. He'll spoil everything.'

Maisy was a word wizard. She liked mixing words together so they turned magic and fizzed into fireworks. Misery. Boots. Splitz!

'There's nothing to spoil,' said Kit and Maisy's dad, giving up trying to fasten his smart tie and letting their mum do it instead. 'As soon as we're out of the house, Alice is putting you straight to bed, aren't you, Alice?'

Alice smiled and rubbed a careful finger, *criss cross criss*, like that, over the scorch mark on her leather school-bag. It looked like a pattern of tiny stars.

'Please tell Joe's mum it will be fine,' she said.

So a few minutes later Joe's mum arrived from next door with Joe and Joe's overnight things. Neither of them looked very happy. Even in her party clothes, Joe's mum looked pale and worried under her smile and Joe just scowled.

Joe was the kind of boy who wore everything tucked in. His trousers were tucked into his socks. His jumper was tucked into his trousers and his shirt was buttoned so high it seemed to reach right up to his ears. He looked like a bulgy Christmas cracker just waiting to be pulled.

Maisy's fingers itched to be the one to do it. *Bang!* No more grumble-guts Joe.

'You look beautiful, Geraldine,' said Kit and Maisy's mum. 'What a lovely dress.'

For a whole second Joe's mum looked pink and pleased. Then she went back to looking worried. She still hadn't made up her mind. She dithered about in her glittery dress like a beautiful shooting star that had fallen down the chimney by mistake.

'I don't know,' she said. 'I mean, er – Joe has such bad dreams. And he isn't used to sleeping in a strange house.'

'It's not that strange,' said Kit and

Maisy's dad, 'except for Kit and Maisy, of course.'

Kit and Maisy pulled faces at him and he pulled faces back, only worse because he had glasses as well as a bristly beard and could make them do diabolical things.

'If only I could be sure Joe would be all right. He's so sensitive . . .'

'He'll be fine, won't you?' said Kit and Maisy's dad in a hopeful voice, smiling at Joe, who didn't seem to be smiling back. 'Alice is a model babysitter, aren't you, Alice? Alice always copes.'

Alice tidied back a strand of hair that was trying to come out of her shiny plait. 'Of course I do,' she said. 'Don't put the guinea pig down just yet, Maisy, I think Zoom zoomed in through the door with me.'

'Alice,' said Kit and Maisy's mum, 'is a treasure without price. I would trust her to the ends of the earth.'

'But he can't always sleep,' said Joe's mum. 'He needs hot milk and honey when he can't sleep. And sometimes he needs me to look in the cupboard with a torch to make sure there aren't any monst –'

'Mummy!' said Joe furiously. 'That's a secret –'

Even though he looked so angry he had

a small airless kind of voice, as if his mother had washed and ironed it by mistake, thought Maisy, and given it back to him with his underwear.

'I can manage hot milk and honey,' said Alice quietly, 'and a dash of cinnamon sometimes helps. And I always have a torch with me in case of – er – emergencies, so that's no problem.'

'Oh dear,' said Joe's mum unhappily. 'You must all think I'm so silly. But I do hope he'll –'

'Of course he will,' cried everybody at once.

'Just look at Kit and Maisy,' said their dad, laughing. 'They can't wait to get rid of us. I'm beginning to think there's more to Alice than meets the eye. I think Alice keeps a magic circus in her pocket.'

Kit and Maisy tried not to smirk.

Maisy sidled up to her mum and said untruthfully, 'Oh, I'll miss you so much, Mummy. Must you go?'

'Come on,' said Kit and Maisy's mum, who wasn't fooled one bit. 'It's high time you enjoyed yourself for a change, Geraldine.'

'Oh dear,' said Joe's mum unhappily. 'I suppose you're right.' But her glittery evening bag slithered right out of her hands as if it didn't want to go to the dinner dance either. Alice quickly picked it up before anyone else had the chance to move.

'Here you are, Mrs Quail,' she said calmly. 'You really needn't worry about Joe. Everyone uses babysitters sometimes and I promise you, if you leave him with me, I'll make sure he has a very special night out of his own.' Then as she handed back the pretty bag, she looked right into Joe's mum's eyes, and her fingers touched Joe's mum's fingers and for a moment there was the faintest smell of wild violets in the room. And suddenly Geraldine Quail was wearing quite a new expression on her face and she was saying, almost excitedly, 'Well, all right then, I *will* come.'

And she managed to get almost half-way out of the door before she remembered she had forgotten to give Joe a hanky to put in his pyjama pocket, and then she got half-way down the front steps before she remembered that she hadn't left his cough mixture. And she got almost out of the gate before she remembered she hadn't given him a proper goodnight kiss. And then she was really gone.

Alice closed the door and leant on it.

Joe couldn't tell what she was thinking. She looked so calm and sensible she probably wasn't thinking anything. He wished he could kick her very hard. That would put a different expression on her face.

But he was puzzled. He couldn't help noticing that Kit and Maisy were dancing around Alice in a silly, excited kind of way and she was hissing at them to shut up. Alice still hadn't moved away from the door. She was listening.

Sure enough in a moment or two, high-heeled footsteps came clipping back to the front door. The bell rang urgently.

Oh no. Joe was ready to die. It couldn't be.

But Alice (holding the door firmly half-closed to discourage Joe's mum from coming back inside) was already answering Joe's mum's question before she had time to ask it.

'Don't worry,' she said, 'I always make them clean their teeth before they go to bed. And wash behind their ears.'

Joe, Kit and Maisy heard a sigh, then, amazingly, a giggle.

'Oh, Alice,' said Joe's mum, and now she was really laughing. 'You are a reliable girl. You've put my mind at rest. There's only the two of us, you see. Joe and me. I can't help worrying.'

'Of course you can't,' agreed Alice. 'It's

perfectly natural. Just have a lovely evening with Mr and Mrs Robinson and leave
the worrying to someone else for one
night.'

'Thank you, Alice. I think I will.'

And the children heard the footsteps flying down the street, faster and lighter than
they had come. But they didn't move a
muscle until the car door slammed and the
engine roared into life. Then Maisy made a
rude noise.

'Your mum,' she said. 'What a worry
wart! But she's ever so pretty. I bet she'll
dance every dance, don't you?' And she
began to waltz around, humming,
pretending her moth-holey sack was a
glittery ball dress.

Joe just scowled. He scowled at his
tightly laced trainers. He scowled at marmaladey, moth-eaten Maisy Robinson and he
scowled at her brother Kit, whose socks
were flying off the ends of his toes like grey
woolly wings and whose very face spelled
trouble. But most of all he scowled at Alice
Fazackerly, the perfect babysitter.

And when he opened his mouth, his voice
didn't just sound washed and ironed. It
sounded as if he kept it in a sardine tin. A
small, flat, whiny voice. A *fishy* voice, where
a boy's voice ought to be. Joe was frightened

and when he was frightened he always got angry so it wouldn't show.

'I never wanted to come here,' he said. 'I hate all of you.' He folded his arms. No one looked at all impressed and that made him feel more scared than ever. '"A very special night out of his own,"' he mimicked. 'That's a laugh! This is going to be the most boring night of my life.'

Kit opened his mouth to say something but Alice shushed him. She was looking interested.

'None of you knows how to have fun,' shouted Joe getting wilder and wilder in his need to make Kit, Maisy and Alice feel as silly as *he* felt. 'None of you has ever even had – had an adventure.'

'Oh,' said Alice politely. 'How can you be so sure?'

'Joe,' interrupted Maisy. 'You don't understand. Alice isn't what –'

'That's okay, Maisy,' said Alice. 'Let Joe explain what he means. Tell us, Joe.'

Suddenly Joe was almost enjoying himself. He'd never been invited to speak his mind before. He was going to make the most of it. 'Anyone can tell as soon as they look at you. You're as boring as – as – school rice pudding. That's why you're in here babysitting instead of out having fun like a real teenager. I bet the most exciting thing you've ever done is play noughts and crosses. And Kit and Maisy are a pair of drips. Their clothes all come from Oxfam. They haven't even got a video.'

Kit went red with rage. He'd been trying to get his mum and dad to buy a video for months. 'Well,' he spluttered, 'my dad told my mum that you were just a spoilt little —'

'That's enough,' said Alice. 'Don't get upset, Maisy. There's no time to lose. Listen you two —' she lowered her voice. 'I've had a message. It has to be tonight.'

Maisy gave a little shriek. 'But what about —' Her eyes swivelled round to Joe who was trying to look bored and superior.

'He'll have to come too.'

'But he'll ruin it,' said Kit. 'He'd be useless. He can't climb or swim or even run. I saw him in the school sports.'

'Hey,' said Joe angrily. 'What's all the whispering? You'd better treat me properly or I'm telling my mum when she comes home.'

He was scared again. What was all this stuff about climbing and swimming? *What* would Joe be useless at?

'Joe,' said Alice sternly. 'Stop huffing and puffing like a dinosaur. I've got something to tell you and we haven't got long. There's a life at stake and we need your help.'

Joe's eyes nearly popped out of his head.

'You see,' said Alice, reaching up her hand and doing something twiddly to her hair so that it tumbled down all around her shoulders, 'there really is more to me —' (she unfastened her leather bag and took out some strange-looking garments, and swiftly slid them on) 'than meets the eye,' she finished up, not even out of breath.

Then she took something else out of her sensible bag.

Joe swallowed.

It was a pistol.

Then she fished out another one and jammed them both in her belt. Then she grinned at Joe.

'Surprised?' she asked.

Surprised was not the word. He was reeling with shock. Where was Alice Fazackerly the perfect babysitter? In front of him stood another person entirely. A girl flaming colours like a tree in autumn. A girl as wild and beautiful as a fairy tale, a moonstone shimmering on her forehead like a fallen star, her hair making a dark storm around her head and shoulders. This was a girl made for danger as sure as fishes swim in the sea.

'Who *are* you?' he spluttered.

'Ah,' said Alice gently. 'That's harder to explain. It's easier to show you. Come across to the window.'

To his surprise Joe found himself doing what he was asked. He knelt up on the window seat and looked out through the curtains.

It was dusk but not yet properly dark. He peered out at the tall, thin terraced houses. What did he see? He saw Alice's bottle-green bike propped against the wall. He saw a ragged old man walking slowly down the street with his collar turned up against the east wind. Then he saw a boy in pyjamas glaring out of an upstairs window and quickly looked away – Kevin Kitchener, his arch enemy. Kevin Kitchener who loved to bully, tease, torment and make your life misery if he decided that you were the wrong kind of boy. Joe was absolutely the wrong kind of boy.

He let a car or two go past with their lights on, before he felt able to say, acting bored: 'What am I supposed to be looking at, exactly?'

Alice rummaged in a pocket. 'Here,' she said. 'Kit and Maisy have theirs already. Put them on and look again.'

Suspiciously Joe opened the small soft bag.

How had Alice known he was coming when he hadn't known himself until a few minutes ago?

A pair of spectacles fell into his hands. The frames were gold wire. The lenses were

the strangest Joe had ever seen. Milky, silvery-pale, with tiny forked lightnings that came and went. They didn't look quite solid; not so much like glass as like frozen moonlight that might unfreeze at any moment and change into something else.

Joe's fingers felt trembly and clumsy. The glasses were so delicate he was afraid he'd damage them. And Kit and Maisy were looking at him as if they didn't like him very much. As if they wished he wasn't there. He had said all those things. He supposed they'd never like him now. He didn't really blame them. He was the wrong kind of boy. People knew it as soon as they set eyes on him.

And then he said, 'Oh.'

Because, once he had them on, the spectacles vanished. They had no weight at all. He couldn't feel them on his nose and when he groped around his face he couldn't tell if they were still there.

And then he said, 'Oh, I don't believe it. Where's – what's – oh, it's *beautiful*. What is it? What's happened? Everything's *different*!'

'It's simple, really,' said Alice Fazackerly quietly at his side. 'It's the Kingdom of Afterdark. And I am the last princess.'

Chapter Two
Moonglasses

Outside the window, the street with its tall thin houses had vanished. In its place were trees; ancient, beautiful, mysterious trees that grew taller and wider than any trees Joe had ever imagined. Trees with danger or magic lurking just behind them. Trees that belonged in a fairy tale.

Where Joe had just seen cars glide by through a rain of autumn leaves, a green river flowed fast, bubbling over stones. And it was no longer dusk. Everything was drenched with light like the brightest summer day.

'Is this real?' Joe breathed. 'Is it truly really real?'

'Of course,' said Alice. 'And once you have put moonglasses on you never forget. It's just that most people think there's only what they see with their ordinary eyes. They don't realise that even the name, Forest Street, is a clue to the magic world secretly tucked inside the ordinary one like a pea in a pod. They don't know about the *Street Forest* and they wouldn't want to. It's a funny thing, I don't know why, most people don't care for sorcery and danger.'

'No,' said Joe, swallowing. 'I suppose not.'

Sorcery and danger.

The palms of his hands felt clammy suddenly as if they had chosen this moment to learn how to rain.

Then he said, more politely than he had ever spoken to anyone: 'Can I take these glasses off now? Thank you very much for showing me, Alice, but I think it must be nearly bedtime. Could you make my hot milk and honey, please?'

He began fumbling at his face. It was very hard to take off a pair of spectacles you couldn't feel. In fact, he discovered, with a wave of panic, it was impossible.

They wouldn't come off!

Behind him Kit and Maisy seemed to be trying not to laugh.

'You've got to help me,' he said angrily. 'I told you. I've had enough. I want to go to bed.'

Then he gasped.

Amongst the trees was a pair of eyes burning like twin fiery coals.

Sorcery and danger!

Joe didn't blame people for not caring much for them. He didn't care for them either. What he wanted most in the world at this moment, was to be bored and bad-tempered in front of the TV. He wanted milk and honey and his own familiar bed. He wished he had never set eyes on Alice Fazackerly.

'I'll tell my mum of you, Alice,' he almost wept. 'Take them off.'

'I'm sorry, Joe,' said Alice very gently. 'I'm afraid that's not possible. We're in a hurry. I told you. Someone's life is at stake.'

'Turn round, Joe,' said Maisy. 'Turn round and look at us, properly.'

Still scrubbing frantically at his face, trying to unpeel the invisible pair of magic moonglasses, Joe reluctantly turned around. His jaw dropped.

The worst thing of all.

Kit and Maisy's house had disappeared.

All the furniture had gone. The bookshelves, Kit and Maisy's crayons scattered on the rug, the rug itself, the guinea pig cage, Joe's overnight bag – the room, the whole crowded cosy untidy room had vanished.

He was in – it couldn't be – a castle hall so enormous he had to screw up his eyes to see the furthest walls. Kit and Maisy were sitting on an unpleasant looking rug made of shaggy animal skin (it couldn't be *wolf*?) warming their hands at a great fire that spat and crackled dangerously on an open hearth before it went roaring up a chimney so huge you could have driven a lorry up it.

Kit and Maisy.

Even Kit and Maisy Robinson had vanished. In their place were a boy and girl who belonged in a fairy tale. Wild children in strange clothes of russet and green. Children made for danger like fishes swim in the sea.

'There's more clothes for you in Alice's bag,' said the strange boy in Kit's voice.

'I don't know how she knew you were coming. But Alice always knows everything,' said the strange girl.

And her voice was just the same as marmaladey Maisy's.

'Don't worry,' she added. 'It is a shock at first. If you put your Afterdark things on you'll feel better. I don't know why, but you will.'

'But I want to go home,' wailed Joe. 'I never wanted to come here. I just want to go home. Take me home.'

Alice sighed but there was a sparkling look of amusement in her eyes as if she had guessed all along that Joe would be like this.

'You don't understand, Joe,' she said, gently. 'It can't be done. This isn't a game you stop playing whenever you feel like it. This is the kingdom of Afterdark and like all kingdoms it has its friends and its enemies. When we've done what we came for, we'll take you back home again.'

Perhaps Joe really would not have screamed then if he hadn't seen the same burning eyes he had seen amongst the trees, smouldering outside the window from just a few metres away.

But close up the eyes were the size of

headlamps. And they belonged unmistakably to a real tiger.

The tiger roared. The whole forest quaked. Then with one bound the tiger simply poured itself through the window, golden and lazy as syrup from a hot spoon.

Joe screamed again.

Then with a second terrible roar, the tiger knocked Alice to the ground.

Joe couldn't bear to look and he was still screaming, his eyes tightly closed, when he heard a new sound, no less deafening but more puzzling and then the unmistakable sound of Kit and Maisy *laughing*.

In fury and terror he opened his eyes and found himself staring into a huge puzzled face, soft and golden as a gigantic sunflower. The tiger was purring.

'Zoom,' said Alice, picking herself up and dusting herself down. 'When will you learn?' But she was laughing too.

'Zoom,' said Joe, still backing away. 'But Zoom's a cat. A boring little tabby cat.'

'Ah,' said Alice, 'but cats are free to wander all the worlds at once, didn't you know? Cats see things people don't see and hear things people don't hear. Zoom is like you and Kit and Maisy. He's like me. There's more to him than meets the eye.'

'Like me?' said Joe hopefully. 'What do you mean?'

'No time,' said Alice crisply. 'You'll find out. Quickly, put your things on. I'm expecting news any minute. Then we can go.'

Joe longed to wail in his ironed-flat sardine-tin voice: *Who? Why? Where?*

But something stopped him. It wasn't just that he didn't dare. He didn't know what it was. But it was a new feeling, a very new feeling indeed for grumble-guts Joe. He had never met anyone like Alice before, he thought. How could she be so ordinary and so mysterious at the same time? How did a princess come to live in two worlds at once? Suddenly he wanted to understand everything.

'Who are you really, Alice?' he said. 'What's your name in Afterdark?'

Alice looked back steadily so that Joe lost himself for a while in her clear grey eyes and found himself bounding through moonlight in the shape of a fawn. There was a scent of violets and the rough spiky smell of rosemary. He tasted the wind on his tongue. He saw each sharp shadow. An owl sounded its hunting cry.

Then Alice was saying, 'I have many names in Afterdark, Joe. Perhaps you will learn some of them before you find your way home again.' And her voice brought him back from the dream, and Joe, still half fawn, felt shivery and happy as if he had been given a glimpse through a mysterious doorway that had always been waiting for him to find it.

Then, blinking, entirely a boy again, he obediently did what Alice told him. He didn't ask how Alice managed to fit so many things inside her sensible leather bag, though he wondered about it a great deal. He just put on the shirt and waistcoat and funny rough trousers; fastened on the belt with its buckle patterned with oak leaves and, when Kit handed him the wicked-looking knife, he took it without a murmur, nervously jamming it into the special little pouch-thing that seemed to be intended for it. When he was ready he looked around shyly, afraid they would all laugh.

But everyone was too busy to notice.

Alice was looking at a map. (Those couldn't be bloodstains on it?)

Kit was cleaning a bright, cruel and curvy something (Joe knew it absolutely couldn't be a sword?) with an old rag and a small tin of metal polish.

Maisy was checking off a list on her fingers.

'Rope, bullets, invisible cloak, apples, digestive biscuits, dragon's teeth . . .'

Joe's eyes popped. All these things were coming out of Alice's bag and Maisy was calmly piling them around her on the floor like supermarket groceries.

Alice nodded. 'Good, I remembered everything. Oh – oh, hang on, what's that?'

'This?' Maisy held up a battered book covered in brown paper and peered inside the cover. 'I think it's your maths homework.'

Alice frowned. 'Bother,' she said. 'I came out in too much of a hurry. I brought the wrong book by mistake.'

For the first time, the Princess of Afterdark looked worried.

'What book did you mean to bring?' asked Joe. 'I thought we'd come here to rescue someone.'

Marmaladey Maisy was right, Joe thought. Wearing his Afterdark clothes made him feel much better. This was such a relief that he decided perhaps Alice wasn't as clever as she thought she was, even if her eyes *were* full of moonlight and violets. After all, how could a boring old book possibly help you to rescue someone?

'*The Observer Book of Monsters*,' said Alice. 'I try never to come without it. The Emperor of Nightfall has the habit of getting monsters to do his dirty work for him. Never mind. We'll do the best we can.'

Joe felt himself go pale. The Emperor of Nightfall? Monsters? The words banged in his ears like dreadful gongs.

'The kingdom of Afterdark has friends and enemies,' said Alice. 'You need to know which is which. Not all monsters are enemies but it could be dangerous to make a mistake. Besides, different monsters must be killed in different ways. Dragons, for example, have a special weakness –'

'I don't want to hear,' said Joe faintly, feeling his new bravery drain out of his shoes and down through the floor.

'Didn't you notice that funny mark on Alice's bag?' asked Kit excitedly. 'Robin got Alice out just in time. But its breath scorched the leather. The Warpworm's breath is so cold nothing can live near it. It burns worse than the fiercest fire. It left those star patterns, look –'

'I told you,' said Joe trembling. 'I don't want to hear any –'

The Warpworm.

Its name was enough to make his knees turn to jelly.

Joe thought he was probably going to die.

If it was going to be monsters and

warpworms he might as well have stayed at home. There was a dark, dark cupboard in his bedroom and he'd always known there was a monster in it. A shapeless terrible monster no nightlight or bedtime story could drive away.

Then he realised what Kit had said and, before he could stop himself, asked in a completely new tone of voice, 'Who's Robin?'

For some reason everyone was staring as if he ought to know without being told. And it was true he had a funny feeling as soon as Kit said the name. A tingly sunburst of gold inside his chest, like swallowing fizzy orange too fast from the bottle.

'Well, go on then, who is he?' he demanded. He hated the way Kit and Maisy seemed to know everything. It made him feel silly and sulky.

'Who is he? Robin Green, of course,' said Kit. 'Cosmo's got him.'

'The Lord of the Forest, silly,' said marmaladey Maisy. 'Don't you know anything? It's why we've come.'

'My beloved,' said Alice Fazackerly.

And she actually blushed a tiny bit.

'And he's in mortal da —' she began to say, but before she could finish her sentence there came a loud banging sound, followed by deep, hollow, bell-like donging and everyone jumped out of their skins. Except the Princess of Afterdark and she rushed straight to the window and peered down.

'It's him,' she cried. 'Why has he taken so long! Run down, Joe, and let him in.'

From somewhere in her clothing she produced a huge iron key.

'And don't,' she said, 'be surprised at anything you see.'

Chapter Three

The map-maker

Joe Quail didn't think he could be surprised at anything ever again but whatever he had been expecting when he finally heaved open the castle door, it was certainly *not* what he saw.

Framed by a wild tangle of flowering creeper, was an extremely sensible-looking horse. It was large, and ivory coloured with a faint all-over marbling of green and it had enormous hooves. It was also grasping one end of a bell rope between its teeth and was tugging it vigorously back and forth. When Joe opened the door the horse simply nosed past and went clattering up the stairs in a matter of fact way, striking sparks with its hooves as it went.

Joe took a frightened peep through the castle door. All he could see was a great deal of unfriendly greenery which seemed to be waiting for an opportunity to wrap itself greedily around him, like a bun around a burger. He shut the door again quickly. By the time he was back upstairs, Kit and Maisy were making a fuss of the horse as if they were all old friends. Even Zoom was winding himself back and forth between them, knocking things over, purring like a sunflower full of bees.

'This is Skydancer,' said Alice. 'There's more to him than meets the eye, Joe, but I expect you'll find that out for yourself before too long.'

It seemed to Joe that there was more than enough of Skydancer already. And what a stupid name! Skydancer was all right for a painted horse on a wooden pole, made to waltz around to a hurdy-gurdy tune. But this was the most solid, sensible down-to-earth horse in the world. It had the kind of legs that should have been glued firmly on to each corner of a piano. Frankly, it looked about as capable of waltzing as spreading a pair of gauzy wings and flying through the air.

'I was hoping Skydancer would have news

of Robin,' said Alice. 'But he says no one will tell him anything now. Things are going from bad to worse in the Forest. Everyone's too afraid of Cosmo and his spies.'

'Could someone please tell me who this Cosmo is?' croaked Joe. But he already had that nasty going-down-fast-in-a-lift feeling you get when you know you aren't going to like the answer one bit.

'Cosmo is the wicked Emperor of Nightfall,' said Kit. 'He's trying to conquer the kingdom of Afterdark so he can make it part of his own evil empire and he's nearly done it, too. Afterdark used to be lovely, but now it's almost as dangerous as Nightfall. Cosmo's been trying to capture Alice and Robin for ages, because they are the only people who stand up to him and he can't bear anyone to do that.'

'And he's got Robin?' asked Joe feeling that tingly fizzy-orange sensation again when he said his name.

'Yes,' said Alice. 'The Emperor has kidnapped him and taken him to the Palace of Nightfall and shut him in his dungeons.'

'They say Cosmo's dungeons are full of horrible things to torture people with,' said Kit.

'They say he keeps a creature in there so dark, dreadful and dangerous,' said

Maisy, 'that no one has ever got out alive.'

'So we shall just have to go and rescue him,' said Alice almost as calmly as if she was going to sit down to do her homework. But Joe noticed that she tightened her hands on the pistols at her belt and narrowed her grey eyes, as if she was already imagining aiming at the evil Emperor.

'Isn't that dangerous?' said Joe, who was trembling more than he thought possible. 'Couldn't we wait just a little longer in case it's all a mistake. Maybe Robin will still turn up safe and sound.'

Alice shook her head. 'No, Joe. We can't afford to waste another minute. The Emperor of Nightfall is a deadly enemy who will stop at nothing. You hop up on to Skydancer with Maisy. Kit and I will follow with Zoom.'

Joe didn't need to look into Alice's eyes this time. He knew she really loved Robin and would do anything to save him. Robin must be a very special person, he thought. Kit and Maisy seemed to love him, too. And though Joe had never even met him, he already felt in awe of him. Just hearing his name was like catching a scrap of a wild song and longing to hear it sung all the way through.

He tried to feel angry and jealous, because it felt so lonely, always being the wrong kind of boy, but once again Joe just found himself meekly doing what he was told. To be honest, he was so scared he didn't really feel anything at all, simply clambered numbly up on to Skydancer's back, and grabbed tightly on to his rough, faintly-green ivory mane.

But he only just had time to feel Maisy grab him from behind, (so tight she pinched horribly, Joe thought, badly wanting to pinch back) when, with a terrifying whoosh, he was flying through the air just as if he had been fired out of a cannon. Skydancer had jumped clean out of the upstairs window with Maisy and Joe on his back.

When Joe recovered from the shock, he was still moving at a tremendous rate. Trees were rushing past, branches grabbing greedily at his hair and clothes. In seconds his hands and legs were a maze of painful scratches.

'Where are we going? Where are Kit and Alice?' Joe shouted, utterly terrified.

But the wind snatched his words away so Maisy didn't hear him.

For hours it seemed, Skydancer tore through the Street Forest. Now and again sunlight dazzled through the branches, blinding them, then they were back inside a leafy green so dark and drowning it was like riding along the sea floor.

Yet if Joe wasn't looking through magic moonglasses, what would he see? Tall, thin terraced houses, slate roofs blue with rain. The *Late Stop* supermarket. The iron railings around the little recreation ground with its swings and broken roundabout. The new telephone box. How could so much dangerously enchanted forest fit inside one safe ordinary street? Joe couldn't understand at all.

Once they passed a great silent pool with white lilies floating on it.

Once they heard something calling with such a piercing, lonely sound, Joe's blood ran cold.

Once a fierce face peered down at him through the tangled branches. A wild brown face, its streaming hair crowned with a garland of honeysuckle. It was a dryad, a tree-girl, her eyes clear and cold as rain.

But they didn't see another living soul, not a bird or beast or human being. And they didn't see Kit and Alice.

Not a hair of them.

And they didn't hear them.

Not so much as a whisper.

Again and again Joe craned his neck round to see if they were following on behind. But all he saw was an immense rushing of green, as if the whole forest was washing over them in towering green wave after wave.

After all, if an ordinary street can turn into an enchanted forest, what's to stop an enchanted forest turning into the sea? Joe felt worse and worse. He wanted his own world with its old reliable rules.

'Alice is my babysitter,' he told himself frantically. 'She wouldn't just go off and leave me.'

But he wasn't convinced. For Alice was not plain Alice Fazackerly any longer. She was the wild Princess of Afterdark, with moonlight in her eyes.

Supposing Skydancer kept galloping forever? Supposing he was taking them in the wrong direction? How *would* they get back home? Just as Joe was sure this nightmare journey would go on for ever, a figure stepped out of the trees, and with a deafening delighted whinny, in a great trampling and splattering of mud, Skydancer halted.

'*Robin*,' cried Maisy. 'But we thought the Emperor had got you in his diabolical dungeon.' She scrambled down and hugged the lion-haired boy in green.

'Not me,' said Robin cheerfully. He wasn't handsome in the least; he had too much nose. But there was a brightness and quickness about him that Joe couldn't help admiring. There was a wildness, too. Joe saw it at once. And when Robin smiled Joe felt the golden sunburst of warmth in his own heart, as if his whole self just had to smile back. But he fought it down. *Danger and sorcery*. Joe still didn't want anything to do with either of them.

'But where are Alice and Kit?' asked Robin, looking worried. 'And who's this?'

'Oh, this is just gru – just Joe Quail from next door,' said Maisy vaguely. 'What do you mean where's Alice? Isn't she with you?'

'We were coming to rescue you,' said

Joe angrily. (He knew Maisy had only just stopped herself from saying 'grumble-guts' in time.) 'So what on earth are you doing here?'

'I don't understand,' said Robin. 'Didn't you set off together?'

'I thought they were coming on behind with Zoom,' said Maisy unhappily. 'We were in a hair-raising hurry because we didn't want you to be tortured and terrorised to death in Cosmo's dungeon.'

Robin didn't just go greenish-white when he was worried, his nose got beakier and pinched-looking and he started pacing up and down. 'We've been tricked,' he said. 'The Emperor *wanted* you to think he'd got me shut up in his dungeon. But it's Alice he's really after. Without her, Afterdark wouldn't have the heart to keep fighting. I bet the moment you lot went charging off, some of his spies crept up and grabbed her.'

How was it that he could look so pale and upset and mud-splattered but still be every inch a determined hero? Joe stared at him longingly, wishing he could be like Robin, instead of the wrong kind of boy, instead of scaredy cat, grumble-guts Joe.

'But she had her pistols,' said Joe.

'Pistols are useless against sorcery and enchantment,' said Robin quietly. 'And the Emperor of Nightfall is the cruellest, most cunning enchanter that ever hatched out of darkness. Come on, you two, follow me. You'll need a good meal inside you before you do anything else.' He smiled at them and the smile was amazingly normal in the circumstances.

'Oh, but I'm not hungry,' said Joe quickly. He was far too worried.

And this was the strange thing. Suddenly he wasn't just worried about how poor Joe Quail would get safely home again. He was worried about the last Princess of Afterdark. He remembered the way she had touched his mother's fingers with her own and how the air had smelled briefly of violets. He remembered how he had fallen through the moonlight in Alice's eyes and become a fawn. There was no one like Alice Fazackerly in the wide world. If something terrible happened to her . . . Then Joe found himself remembering Kit, too, and the way his silly socks flew off at the ends of his toes like grey woolly wings. What if he never saw Kit Robinson again?

'I'm a very good cook, you know,' said Robin, matter of factly, moving ahead of them, bright and quick as a deer. 'It's the first rule of being an outlaw. (Well, the second one, after learning to fade into the forest like a green shadow.) Learning how to make a good stew out of practically nothing. So come and try it while we think what to do next.'

'We might as well,' said Maisy. 'We don't know how long it will be before we have another meal.'

She seemed surprisingly calm. Joe supposed she must have become used to danger and sorcery. He didn't *ever* want to get used to them. But he discovered he just couldn't hate Maisy as much as he meant to. He even discovered that he no longer believed the Robinson kids had ganged up against him with their tulip-guzzling rabbit and their gawping giant sunflowers. He had just been jealous because they always seemed to have such a good time. He had been jealous of the careless cheerful way they roared around making as much noise and mess as they possibly could. And he had been jealous, too, of the way Laura, their mum, sang so happily out of tune, and the way their dad teased her about her floury nose.

He slithered from Skydancer's back and trudged thoughtfully through the undergrowth after the others. Robin was extremely hard to follow because he could turn himself so successfully into a green shadow.

When they came out at last into the sunshine, Robin led them uphill along the bank of a fast-flowing stream until they reached a gigantic waterfall suspended magically above them in seven separate waterfalls, each one underneath the other, each one dancing with rainbows.

Then to Joe's surprise, Robin scrambled up the rocks and vanished into the nearest waterfall.

'This bit always gets you so spectacularly splashed,' said Maisy, sighing.

Then she too vanished into the curtain of falling water.

Joe screwed up his eyes (he hated getting cold and wet), scrambled up the slope (he was terrified of climbing), looked wildly around (there was no way he could possibly get out of it), took a deep breath and charged at the waterfall.

The next minute he was in a dry cave comfortably heaped with furs and bracken, with the crystal music of the falling water behind him. Still wobbly with pride and extremely out of breath, he just managed to stop himself walking into the bunches of dried herbs hanging from the roof and socked his head on a smoked ham. Maisy giggled. Towards the back of the cave a gnarled figure was stirring a great black iron stewpot over the fire. Something smelled wonderful.

But Joe couldn't concentrate properly on the cave or the stew. He couldn't take his eyes off the ragged old man who was sprinkling dried herbs into the stew, rubbing each pinch between finger and thumb as carefully as a wizard, before he put it in. And Joe simply couldn't keep quiet.

'I've seen you before,' he blurted out. 'You were walking past the window when Alice told me to look out at the street and tell her what I saw.'

The old man smiled and even in the gloom of the cave Joe could see how bright his eyes were. Like sparks of blue fire.

'Coll doesn't talk,' said Robin. 'He just comes and goes, and watches and listens. You can trust him, Joe. He's a friend. A true friend of Afterdark. You'd better give them some stew,' he said to the old man. 'They'll need it to keep their strength up. We think the Emperor's got Alice.'

The old man silently filled two bowls with stew and handed one to each of the children with hunks of bread. Joe was surprised to find how very hungry he was.

'The trouble is,' said Robin, sitting down by the fire so that light and shadow flickered over the glorious green and lion-gold of him, almost as if he were a tree-person himself, thought Joe, crowned with a shadowy garland of honeysuckle, 'Cosmo's got us well and truly cornered. There were trolls in the forest this morning. I know they're up to something. If we go dashing off to Nightfall after Alice, we could just be playing right into his hands and lose everything we have been fighting for. We can't leave Alice and Kit in his clutches but we daren't leave Afterdark completely undefended.'

'Aren't there any other outlaws who will help you?' asked Joe, who had seen a number of patched cloaks and worn-out boots scattered about the cave. There had to be a band of other young men as wild and daring as Robin, still roaming around somewhere out in the forest?

Robin shook his head. 'The Emperor has picked them off one by one,' he said. 'Coll and I are the only ones left.'

Joe was appalled. Robin looked so tired and unhappy again that Joe wished he hadn't spoken. But even more, he wished with all his heart that *he* could help Robin save the troubled kingdom of Afterdark.

If only he wasn't the wrong kind of boy.

Shyly he said, 'Alice said the Princess of Afterdark has many names.'

'That's true,' agreed Robin. His eyes wandered sadly to a woven tapestry hanging from the rough walls of the cave. Joe couldn't make out the picture very clearly at first through the woodsmoke, just the general moonlighty feel to it, but after a while he thought there was a girl with a storm of hair and a number of dangerous-looking wild animals clustering around her. A hawk-like bird was settling on her wrist. The girl had a pale jewel bound across her forehead and starry rays gleamed from it.

'The Lady of the Beasts,' said Joe, wondering how on earth he knew.

'You're right, Joe. That's one of her names,' said Robin, and he smiled at him so delightedly that again Joe experienced that giddy sunburst inside his chest. 'She told you her first name, Joe, because she knew you were ready to hear it. That's the most hopeful thing that's happened to us today. I wonder – you know I'm beginning to think Alice knows the perfect way to put things right.'

Joe thought Robin was making fun of him. How could Alice possibly tell either of them anything when she was probably imprisoned in a dungeon, hundreds of miles away from here? Yet it was peculiar, the way the words had popped into his mind, as though by magic.

Coll was looking more than usually thoughtful, as if he, too, was listening to words that had popped, like magic rabbits, into his silver-grey head. Suddenly, he rose from his seat by the fire and went to the back of the cave where a number of old chests and boxes were piled higgledy-piggledy. He unlocked the largest, oldest, shadowiest-looking chest of all, locked it carefully again and came back to the fire holding a rolled-up piece of parchment.

'Coll is a map-maker,' said Robin. 'It's hard to explain, Joe, but map-makers are very special people in Afterdark. Almost like magicians. Only the magic isn't theirs to use. A map-maker's special magic is to help other people find and use *their* magic.'

Joe didn't understand this at all but he was tired of seeming stupid so he just nodded and kept his mouth shut tight.

Robin unrolled the map. Spread flat on the floor of the cave, it was the size of a small tablecloth.

'But there's nothing on it,' said Joe, disgustedly. He couldn't help it. He could never trust people for long. He was so afraid someone was trying to make a fool of him.

'Look again, Joe,' said Robin. There was a note of excitement in his voice.

Joe stared.

In front of his astonished eyes, the map began to fill itself in, in vivid singing colours. There was the castle, the tangled forest paths, the dryad's tree, the pool of floating flowers and the place where Robin had stepped out in front of Skydancer. And there was the outlaws' hideout behind the waterfall. It was the map of Joe and Maisy's journey.

But the rest of the map was blank.

'But what use —' Joe began, when Coll grasped his arm fiercely and made him look again.

A wiggly line was racing across the blank map as if drawn by an invisible hand. Other lines chased the first one. Lines that turned into streams, trees and rocky coast-lines. Lines that reared up like impossible mountains. And — Joe choked: monsters. Definitely monsters.

'But I —'

'Look properly,' ordered Robin. 'Don't cheat. Read the writing.'

Joe's ears went red. Reading was not his favourite thing and when he was feeling lazy he preferred to guess. He was such a clever guesser his mother never caught him at it.

He sighed. The writing on the map was difficult but eventually he managed to spell out all the words.

'Here be Monsters,' he said. 'And here ye Ocean beginnes. And here is ye Palace of Nightfall. But it can't be. That's silly. It's in the middle of the sea. It would get wet and rot like an old tree.'

'You've missed this bit,' said Robin. His eyes were sparkling. He had cheered up completely now.

'Oh, that's not fair,' said Maisy who was a fast reader as well as a word wizard. 'Why should grumble-guts Joe have all the fun.'

But Joe's eyes were glued to the map. He had just understood what he was reading.

'A *Faithful Map*,' it said, '*of Joe Quail's Deadly and Dangerous Quest.*'

With a mouth dryer than burnt toast, Joe went on. 'Here Joe encountered Trolls. Here Joe did Battle with Dragons.'

There was more but he wouldn't even look at it.

'This is stupid,' said Joe, getting angry. 'How can it be a map of my journey? Maps don't tell you what is going to happen to you before you go somewhere. They don't tell you that sort of thing at all.'

'Don't they?' asked Robin, flickering green and gold as a beech tree in the firelight. 'Well, I suppose they don't. It doesn't say what the trolls *did* to you or who *won* the battle with the dragons.'

'You don't understand,' said Joe irritably. 'Maps don't tell you what happens. They tell you where the mountains are and the ancient monuments and that sort of thing.'

'Not in Afterdark, they don't,' said Robin. 'And I'm afraid once your name appears on a map like this one you simply have to go out and get on with it. I though we had no choice but to go and rescue Alice together, even if it meant risking the kingdom. But it didn't feel right somehow. You get an instinct for these things after a bit. But the map makes everything perfectly clear.'

'Does it?' quavered Joe. 'Not to me it doesn't.'

'Of course! It means that this is *your* adventure, Joe, and no one else's. If I interfere with this map we might never get Kit and Alice back at all. It means that it's you that will save us, if anyone can. And my task is to stay here with Coll and Maisy and defend what's left of the Forest until Alice is returned to her kingdom. Which means the fate of Afterdark is really in your hands. Finished your stew? Better get going then.

Skydancer will be waiting for you. Take an apple for him if you like.'

'But I don't know where to – I –'

'Don't forget the map,' said Robin, clapping him on the shoulder. 'Have you got a sword? I thought not. But Alice has given you a knife? A knife can be quite deadly enough if you're really desperate. You'll just have to keep your wits about you. Good luck, Joe.'

'Good luck, Joe,' echoed marmaladey Maisy, who looked as surprised and scared as Joe at the way things were turning out.

'What will you do, Maisy?' asked Joe, his voice wobbling.

Maisy gave a little shrug and tried to smile. 'I'll keep a look out for spies,' she said bravely. 'It won't be the first time.' Then Maisy reached out and squeezed his hand, pinching hard, the sort of squeeze you give a friend, who is going to need all his courage. Joe was so shocked he squeezed her hand right back, before he had time to think.

Then before he knew what was happening he was stumbling away from the waterfall, with a windfall apple in his pocket and the map of Joe Quail's Deadly and Dangerous Quest tucked under his arm.

Skydancer was waiting for him as Robin

had promised, and stood quietly grazing as Joe clambered awkwardly on to his back.

'This is dreadful,' said Joe, trying not to cry. 'This isn't fair. They can't make me, you know.'

But even as he spoke he knew his whiny words were lies, spoken out of old habit and that it was Coll's mysterious map which was true. Even though Joe was the kind of boy who felt sick on buses and turned blue with fear every time he went to the swimming baths, all his life he had secretly dreamed of being the hero of a real adventure. And now, as if he had magnetised it to him through wanting it so much, a real adventure had actually tracked him down like a wolf in the forest and Joe had to follow it. There was almost a relief in knowing he had no choice.

'The fate of Afterdark is in your hands,' he repeated hoarsely.

Joe was scared to death. He was shaking like a leaf. He was shaking, he thought, (pretending to be Maisy for a minute or two) like a thousand leaves in a hurricane.

But for the first time in his life, Joe Quail wouldn't have changed places with anybody.

Chapter Four
Dragonfire

Sometimes as Joe sped along on Skydancer's back he wondered what his mother would say if she could see him now. He imagined riding up to the posh hotel where she was at the dinner dance with the Robinsons and sweeping her up in front of him in her glittery dress. Only a few hours ago she was fussing over his cough mixture and here he was, scarcely recognisable as the same Joe, with nothing but a knife, a magic map and a withered apple between himself and danger.

Now and again he made Skydancer stop so he could look at the map to see how they were getting along. A new wiggly line had sprung up beside the place called Robin's Hideout. They were still a long way from the sea.

Joe tried not to think about the sea. He hated water as much as he hated the dark. All water. Puddles, canals, swimming pools. But worst of all was the sea which was never settled or satisfied, rushing at him thirstily as though to swallow him for ever.

He smelled the trolls before he saw them. Skydancer reared in disgust. They smelled worse than the town dump. They smelled worse than the glue factory. And then he saw them and they looked every bit as bad as they smelled. There were only five of them but they were large ones, with big stupid faces and big red hands like joints of beef.

Joe was so frightened that for the first time in his life he did the right thing. He stayed exactly where he was with the sun behind him so that it dazzled the trolls' weak, red-rimmed eyes.

And he didn't wait to be spoken to. He spoke. And he didn't speak in his own voice. He thought of the most frightening person he knew, who was Mr Dawlish, the P.E. teacher at Golden Street Juniors, and he made himself sound as much like him as he could.

'Hey,' he bawled at them, wildly trying
to imagine himself bald and bony in a baggy
old purple tracksuit. 'What on earth do you
think *you're* doing? Does the Emperor know
you're here?'

The biggest troll turned slowly to face
him. Trolls do everything slowly, except
for eating, which they do remarkably fast
because of not bothering to chew.

'Who wants to know?' said the troll,
stupidly peering into the glare. 'Eh? Eh?
Who wants to know?'

'Cosmo does,' said Joe, trying to make
his voice sound even bigger and more
dangerous. Mr Dawlish wasn't a big man
but his voice gave people headaches for miles
around.

'And what business is that of yours? Eh?'

The troll looked sly and suspicious but that was probably just how troll faces looked. Mr Dawlish had to sort out kids who looked worse than that every day.

'Very important business,' said Joe, hoping the troll couldn't see the bits of him that were shaking. 'I work for him. And I don't want anyone to let him down. Cosmo doesn't like anyone to let him down.'

'That's true,' said a smaller troll squinting through the sunlight. 'He doesn't. He's an evil bloke to cross, that Emperor. But you needn't go telling on us because we're only making sure none of that slimy Afterdark bunch are creeping about. He doesn't want them spoiling his chances at the last moment, Cosmo doesn't.'

'Well, make a proper job of it,' said Joe, 'or I'll make sure he gets to hear of it.'

He clicked his tongue to Skydancer to tell him to walk on and rode steadily past, all the time keeping directly in the blinding sunlight so that all the trolls ever saw of Joe was a great, dark figure on a great, dark horse.

'He's a flaming hard bloke to please, that Emperor,' Joe heard one mutter as he passed. 'Hasn't got a trusting bone in his body.

Sending out his spies to spy on *us*. Eh? What about that? Cunning bloke, though. Have to admire him. Keeps us on our toes from morning till night. Never sleeps.'

Joe couldn't believe it. Though he knew trolls are stupid and easily fooled, he also knew they are extremely dangerous. He had been in real danger. But he had kept his head. He wished Kit and Maisy had been there to see him. Or Alice Fazackerly. Or my mum, he thought.

He must try to remember that trick about pretending to be Mr Dawlish. Perhaps, if he ever got back home, he could try it out on Kevin Kitchener. He had felt fierce and strong. He had even felt taller. And not scared at all. Well, not much.

But Joe's high spirits didn't last long. They never did. And pretty soon his heart sank right back into the bottom of his boots, as he remembered what the magic map appeared to be planning for him.

'Dragons next,' he said to himself, full of dread.

Dragons were tougher customers than trolls. Dragons are cunning brutes with long, dark memories. Joe knew he'd have to think of something cleverer than keeping in the sunlight and pretending to be his own P.E. teacher.

I can't fool a dragon. But I absolutely
know I can't fight one, either, he thought.
But the map was positive that Joe did *battle*
with dragons. Joe took it out and had
another look to make quite sure. (He also
peered very hard in case there wasn't really
an S on the end of dragons, but only a
smudge or spot of spilled stew. It was an S,
of course.)

He had to fight. He didn't have a choice.
But I can't.

Joe was scared again. His hands were
sweaty. His heart bumped.

I *can't* fight a dragon. Not even a small
one. I might as well give up. He had to
turn back. But that meant going back to
Robin and Maisy and silent Coll the map-
maker and admitting what a coward he was.

He couldn't do that either. By now
Cosmo might be torturing Kit and Alice
in his dungeons. If Joe didn't save them
something terrible would happen to them.

'The fate of the kingdom of Afterdark is
in your hands,' Robin had said.

'Oh, I do wish it wasn't,' sighed poor
Joe.

For the last few minutes Skydancer had
been picking his way carefully up a steep
stony hillside. A smoky haze hung in the
air as if someone somewhere was burning

leaves. Sometimes the horse stumbled slightly on the larger stones. After this had happened rather too often for comfort, Joe took a closer look.

His scalp shrank with fear.

They were not stones but skulls.

Then he realised the smoke was not from a gardener's bonfire. It couldn't be. There were no trees or bushes anywhere. There wasn't even a blade of grass. The landscape was as bleak and bare as a bone. Without knowing it, Joe had ridden into dragon country.

It was *dragonfire*.

Dragons don't improve the countryside. They lay waste to it. Burn, batter and blast every living thing in sight. Then, of course, there's nothing left to do and they feel dreadfully bored and depressed. Dragons are notoriously touchy, bad-tempered brutes. There is always a horrible atmosphere in dragon country. Like a war just waiting to happen.

Joe was on top of the hill now, looking across stony little hills shaped rather like wizards' hats. The valley below him was dotted with caves and it was out of these that the thick, green smoke came coiling and curling.

Joe hurriedly counted at least thirteen

caves. Thirteen dragons if there was one to each cave. But what if there was a whole *family* of dragons to each one? Or more? He wished he had a copy of *The Observer Book of Monsters* with him, so he could look up dragon habits in it.

Oh, for goodness sake, he scolded himself. What does it matter, how many dragons there are? They can only kill me once.

Joe was suddenly utterly sick of being scared of everything. Not just sick of being scared of dreadful things like trolls and dragons, but being so scared of *everything*. Like school swimming, or being beaten up by Kevin Kitchener and made to eat school cabbage by the dinner lady with a witchy whisker on her chin.

Joe Quail had had enough.

Being a full-time scaredy cat took up too much room inside his head. It took up too much room inside his life. For years Joe had never managed to get a good night's sleep for worrying what dark, shapeless thing was going to creep out of the cupboard and ooze across to his bed, the moment he closed his eyes.

Joe had a new thought. An even better one. Maybe when you are really and truly sick of something, you *actually stop doing it*.

'We'll stay up here for a while, Sky-dancer,' he said. 'To give ourselves time to think up a good plan.'

But secretly he wanted to hold on to the encouraging thought a little while longer.

He slid off Skydancer's back and looked around him. He didn't like what he saw.

'Why do you think the Emperor of Night-fall wants to conquer Afterdark so badly?' he said aloud. 'I haven't seen a single friendly bit of it yet. Perhaps it used to be nice before. Perhaps it would even be nice again if we could stop the Emperor trampling all over it. It can't just be full of monsters and torture-things. Alice and Robin and Coll can't be the only nice people here.'

For some reason this thought made him feel better. In fact, when he put this thought together with the other new thoughts, he probably felt about as good as it is possible for a boy to feel, alone on a skull-strewn hillside, waiting to be slain by an unknown number of dragons.

He was hungry, he realised. It was a long time since Robin's stew. All he had in his pockets was the apple Robin had given him for Skydancer. He sighed. He was very hungry indeed and growing hungrier every minute, but he knew it just wouldn't be fair of him to eat the windfall.

'Go on,' he said, holding it out bravely. 'You'd better have it. Robin meant it for you and you've been carrying me on your back for hours. You must be starving. I won't die from hunger yet.'

Skydancer stretched his great head forward and took most of the apple ungratefully in two loud crunchy bites from Joe's hand, while Joe tried not to mind too much about the enormous yellow teeth.

'Oh, don't you want the core?' he said disgustedly. 'Well, I certainly don't.'

And he threw the apple core away from him down the hillside, wiping his sticky hands on his clothes.

And then he said, 'Oh.' And then he said, 'Oh, sorry, I never meant –'

For the apple core was gathering speed hurtling downhill and as it went it bumped into all kinds of other objects on the way down; pebbles, rocks, skulls so that they, too, were launched into motion and went bowling away down the echoing, hollow slopes like marbles in a gigantic marble run.

Before Joe could leap on to Skydancer's back and gallop guiltily away, half the hillside was already sliding away from him with a vast sucking, gritty rush and roar, and dragons everywhere were sticking their bald, scaly heads out of caves, bellowing with rage.

Then the battle began, the battle of the dragons.

It was low cunning against high cunning. Fang against claw. Green fire against gold fire. Scarlet against blue. It went on for hours and hours and hours. Until at last there was no fire at all, only smoke. Thick black oily smoke.

And silence.

What could Joe do except stay out of the way on his bare and lonely hilltop, trying not to look, trying not to listen? All he had done was throw away a single apple core, but that was enough to make each of the bored, angry dragons think the other dragons had deliberately started a landslide.

It couldn't have worked out better if he had planned it. But he hadn't planned it and he felt awful. He didn't feel clever or even a little bit pleased with himself. How could a single innocent apple core do so much harm? When they were quite sure it was really over, Joe and Skydancer rode away.

They travelled on until they left the

stony, wizard's-hat hills with their dark, dragon smoke far behind and crossed into greener, gentler country. Joe Quail had outwitted the trolls and defeated the dragons, even if he had only defeated them by mistake. But the most dangerous part of the quest was still to come.

Chapter Five

The door in the water

It was getting late. The shadows across the water meadows were growing long and spindly. The streams were full of marsh marigolds. Joe saw a heron daydreaming on one leg. He thought he heard the cry of a gull. He even thought he could smell the sea. But he still felt so dreadful it was hard to think about anything else. He felt sick every time he thought about the battle of the dragons. The way their fury turned the air a sullen red all around, like a bloodshot eye. And then all those dragons lying dead, staring emptily at the sky, and the oily black smoke coiling around the hills like the end of the world.

'I never meant that to happen,' he said to Skydancer, since there was no one else to talk to and he was growing fond of the horse. 'I know they would have eaten me if they'd had the chance. Why doesn't that make me feel better?'

And then he said, crossly, 'Oh no, now what?' For they really had reached the glinting restless edge of the sea at last and he realised he had not just been putting off thinking about this because he was afraid of so much thirsty water but because, deep down, he had known all along there was absolutely no way for Skydancer to cross it.

No bridge, no causeway. No ferry, not even a raft to carry them across. And it was miles too far to swim even for a really good swimmer like Maisy Robinson.

And rising up, far and away in the dizzy middle of the foaming ocean, mocking him, was the beautiful, impossible, many-coloured palace with impossible cloud-capped towers that soared like an enchanter's dreams towards the stars.

The Palace of Nightfall.

And Joe knew he would never save Kit and Alice now. He had failed in his quest after all and he had failed for the simple reason that he was, always had been, and always would be, absolutely the *wrong* kind of boy.

For a long time he looked out over the water's edge. It was curiously hard to take his eyes away from Cosmo's palace. He wondered if he should take another look at the map. Maybe it could tell him what was meant to happen next. But that didn't feel like the right thing to do this time. Then he heard Skydancer scrunching hopefully at a dry clump of grasses and rubbed the horse's ears to comfort himself.

'Oh, Skydancer,' said Joe, his eyes stinging. 'You've brought me so far. I wish you *did* have wings then we really could rescue Alice and Kit.'

At this Skydancer turned and gave Joe a long tired look and then he sighed, a huge tired horse sigh, as if to say: of course you would leave it right until the last minute before you thought of it.

Then, with a crisp downy rush, like a whole flight of swans taking off, the horse unfurled two faintly green-marbled wings, quivered them just enough to shake the stiffness out, then soaring into the air with astonishing grace, Skydancer began to speed through the sunset towards Cosmo's magical palace in the sea.

'Oh, Skydancer, there really is more to

you than meets the eye,' said Joe, enchanted at finding clouds streaked like raspberry-ripple ice cream, brushing past his ears and tangling around his shoe laces.

The horse gave him another odd look, almost as if it wanted to laugh, Joe thought, but he was too excited to think about it much. He was even too excited to remember to be afraid.

The nearer he got to the palace, the more beautiful, magical and impossible it seemed. It was many-coloured but the colours were the deep, quiet colours of twilight, washing into one another like wet water paints. All the towers were twirly at the tops like genies' turbans and they were reached by dizzy, delicate stairways of shining stuff. Almost every part of Cosmo's palace seemed to be trying to fly or hover or reach the stars. Even the fantastic gardens seemed to float in the air and aerial fountains gushed rainbows of sunlit spray over everything.

'But I thought the Emperor was an evil person,' said Joe, puzzled.

How could anyone as cruel and wicked as Cosmo build such a beautiful palace?

And now he could hear music. Soft music blowing across the water.

'I must concentrate,' said Joe, realising

he was getting carried away by the wonder of it all. 'I must think about what to do next. Where will they be? In the dungeon? However will I find it?'

Suddenly Joe realised Skydancer was spiralling in to land.

'What are you doing? You can't just stop here,' he protested.

But Skydancer had. They had come to rest on a rock only just wide enough for Skydancer's hooves. A rock so close to the back entrance of the palace that from it Joe could see a dark narrow doorway half in and half out of the sea.

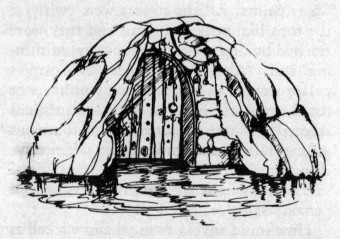

He shivered and understood from his turned-to-jelly knees that this was the doorway to the dreadful dungeon.

'But I can't get across to that,' said Joe,

really scared just when he had been so sure he would never be frightened again. 'I'm a terrible swimmer. Mr Dawlish says I'm hopeless. I'll drown.'

But he was almost at the end of his quest. Was he going to throw it all away just because he was frightened of swimming a few feeble metres in a perfectly calm sea? Yes, he thought. There are some things that are just too dangerous. Swimming, when you truly couldn't, was one of them.

Then Joe heard a cry, so lonely and full of terror he went cold all over and then colder still. Was that Kit? Was it Alice? Was Cosmo torturing them?

Joe discovered he had climbed down without knowing it. There was only just enough room for him to balance.

'Oh dear,' he said, tottering on the edge of the water, fixing his eyes unhappily on that blind, dreadful door, half in, half out of the sea. Then in his head he said fiercely, 'I am coming, Alice, honestly I am,' and aloud he moaned, 'Oh, here goes, oh *help*!'

And holding his nose, he dived, and to his astonishment found himself *swimming* strongly through warm water, swimming like a fish, swimming as though he had swum every day of his life. If swimming was really this easy, this glorious, why ever hadn't he done it before?

When he reached the dungeon doorway he was almost sorry he didn't have further to go, he felt so proud of himself. For a second he clung to the rusty handle of the underwater door, shaking the water out of his eyes and ears, then he turned to grin at Skydancer.

The rock was empty. The flying horse had vanished.

No use thinking about that, thought Joe, his teeth chattering. No use at all. Remember what you're here for. Got to get Alice and Kit out of the dungeon. Twist the knob. Take a deep breath and go in.

Easier said than done. This couldn't be the main door to Cosmo's dungeons. It was stiff, rusted solid with years of sea salt. There were fronds of seaweed growing around it and little shells and barnacles and sea anemones stuck to it.

At last, summoning all his strength, Joe gave a mighty shove. With the ghastly groan of an outraged ghost, the door opened inwards and Joe swam into total darkness.

The door slammed.

Perhaps the sea had forced it shut. It hardly mattered.

He was trapped in the dark, underwater.

Then he heard it again. That lost cry. It sounded closer. Joe splashed along blindly, terrified of what he might meet but not knowing what else to do.

'Is that you, Alice?' he called, trying not to swallow salt water. 'Is that you?'

Then he heard the voice again. The terrified, inhuman voice. Only this time it used words.

'No-o,' it wailed. 'It's me-ee. But please don't hurt me. Just answer the riddle and I'll let you go-o. That's the rule. I didn't make it but I have to obey it just the same. One riddle and then they can go. Of course they don't ever go because they can never tell me the answer and then they fight and scream. Then they go quiet.' The voice sniffled. 'I hate it when they go quiet,' it wept.

Whatever it was, Joe decided it must have something very wrong with it. It was wheezing away like an old accordion.

Joe peered through the dark, straining his eyes to see. It was too dreadful for words, being trapped in the dark with an invisible something that wheezed, sniffled and wailed.

But to his surprise he found he was terribly sorry for whatever it was. It was the loneliest thing he had ever met in his life.

'Has Cosmo shut you down here?' he asked.

'Don't!' shrieked the thing in terror. 'He has spies everywhere. I mustn't tell you. Just answer the riddle and I'll let you go.'

'But no one ever answers the riddle,' Joe pointed out. 'You just said so. And if I can't answer it, you can't let me go.'

'Oh, don't muddle me,' wept the thing. 'Just try to answer the riddle. Answer the riddle and I'll let you go.'

Then Joe realised that the thing had been shut down here in the darkness for so long it had almost lost its wits. All it could do was repeat what it had been told and it could only do that because someone had frightened it so badly it was terrified of forgetting its words and being punished.

'Come on then,' Joe sighed. 'Ask me the riddle if it makes you feel better.'

There was a puzzled silence, as if no one had cared about the invisible thing's feelings before. Then it made a throat clearing sound and began in a wobbly sing-song:

'You will find me in darkness
and also at night. Especially
When you are alone and terribly fright
-ened. If you open the door

I never come out. (Ha ha.) But if you
  leave it shut
you can't be sure I'm not still hiding in
  there somewhere.'

'That's it,' said the thing. 'I think,' it
added in a worried voice. 'I didn't write it.
He did,' it explained. 'I have to say it just
like he tells me.'

'It isn't a very good riddle,' said Joe. He
didn't know whether to laugh or cry. It was
a terrible riddle. But the most terrible part
of all was that he knew the answer to it as
well as he knew his own name. Which
meant he knew exactly *what* was trapped
down here in the dark with him.

He swallowed. Why was there always
something left to be scared of? He had sur-
vived trolls and dragons. He had flown
through the air and swum through the sea.
He had even crawled into this underwater
dungeon to rescue his friends. But he might
as well have stayed at home. The worst terrors
are the ones without shapes. The ones without names. The ones inside your own head.

It was Joe's turn to clear his throat.

'You're a monster,' he said. 'And you're
not just any old monster. You're *my* monster, aren't you?'

There was a short silence. Then there was

a wheezy sigh followed by some sniffing and something that might have been a sob. Then a disbelieving voice said: 'Would you just say that again, please? In case I made a mistake. Sometimes I get water in my, er —'

'You're my monster,' said Joe in a louder voice. 'I know you are, so you needn't pretend. Now I suppose you'll eat me up.'

There was a faint scratching sound. 'Sorry,' said the voice, much closer this time. 'They're a bit damp.'

Joe shielded his eyes. A yellow flower of light floated in front of him. He could make out a bulky, bluish shape, a small head with frondy bits on it, like something you might find on a very old lady's hat, and a pair of pale peering eyes.

'I'm very ugly, aren't I?' said the voice. 'Don't worry you'll offend me by screaming. I know I'm ugly.'

'You aren't as bad as all that,' said Joe bravely. 'Not that bad at all, really.'

'The damp doesn't do me any good,' said the monster sadly. 'I'm a nicer colour when I'm dry. At least I think so. To tell you the truth I can't properly remember what I'm supposed to look like any more. I don't know if I was always like this. The feet don't seem quite —'

It vanished with a little cry of pain as

the match went out, burning its bluish jelly fingers. When it reappeared it was smiling, a lit match flowering in each hand. 'I'll show you the way out, if you like,' it said. 'It's a much nicer door than the one you came in by.'

It was. The monster only had to use four matches to get them there. There were some steps, high and curving and at the top was the door which was wide and well above the water level. It must also have been well oiled because the monster got it open without any trouble. Soft air and light came flooding in and with it the faint music Joe had heard before.

'You're letting me go?' said Joe.

'Of course,' said the monster. 'You answered the riddle. That means you've tamed me and I can't hurt you. It's the rule.'

'So what happens to *you*?' asked Joe.

The monster looked puzzled. It was still shielding its eyes from the light. And it was changing colour, Joe noticed, its bluish skin drying in the air from the open door. It looked healthier already and wasn't wheezing so much. Maybe monsters recover quickly.

'I don't know. He never told me,' it said. 'Do you think I can go?' Its jelly paws were trembling. 'Do you think it's all right for me to go out yet, even if my feet aren't quite –' It was twisting round, trying to see itself better.

'I think you should,' said Joe. 'It's not good for you being shut down here. Can you tell me how to find Kit and Alice?'

The monster crinkled up its forehead in a baffled kind of way, the way a baby might.

'My friends,' explained Joe. 'Kit Robinson and Alice. Only Alice is really the Princess of Afterdark.'

The monster went so quiet for so long that Joe became horribly convinced that Cosmo had already killed them, but before he could open his mouth again to panic aloud, the monster sighed a deep sigh, like someone waking from a long frightening dream to find himself safe after all in his own bed, in his own home.

'The Princess,' it said softly. 'The Afterdark Princess. I knew her when she was only a little . . .'

'You *knew* her!' said Joe excitedly. 'The Lady of the Beasts?'

After all, the monster was a *kind* of beast, Joe thought.

'Of course I know her but somehow I had forgotten . . .' Its voice trailed off as if it was remembering other things long, long ago.

'Well, where are they? Are they in Cosmo's other dungeons?' Joe asked impatiently. The monster was wearing such a dreamy, far-away expression Joe was afraid it had forgotten he was there.

The monster shook his head, sternly shaking the last wisps of dreaminess out. 'There is only one dungeon,' he said, in a new, brisker tone of voice. 'And it was only ever *meant* to be a wine cellar. So cool, you see. No, if your friends are still here, they'll be shut up in the Glass Tower. *That* was really meant for the observatory. It's only the top part that's glass. Go along the corridor until you reach the banqueting hall, then climb the Shining Stair and you'll find them.'

Its eyes looked different, Joe thought. No longer hurt and clouded. Perhaps its wits were returning after its long imprisonment. But he did wonder how the monster knew its way around Cosmo's palace so well. Perhaps it had taken the chance to have a good snoop around before Cosmo shut it in the dungeon to frighten people.

'Here, take this. I seem to have got a spare one. I can't remember why.'

The monster was pushing something small and hard into Joe's hand. 'You'll need it. But do be careful. Cosmo will be looking for you now.'

'Don't worry,' said Joe, politely putting whatever it was the monster had given him into his pocket without looking at it. It felt like a stone or a shell. Perhaps the monster collected them. 'I'll be fine now. Honestly.'

But when Joe turned, a minute or so later, the monster was still anxiously watching him out of its great, pale eyes.

'Hey,' Joe called impulsively. 'Do *you* know any of her other names? The Princess, I mean.'

'Do you mean the Daughter of All Directions?' the monster called back. 'That is one. And once you know it you can never be lost in the dark again and the wind will turn itself round for you.'

It licked a dim blue finger and held it up, then looked quite comically perplexed, as if it had only just remembered the name itself and couldn't understand how it could have forgotten such a strong piece of magic.

'Thank you,' said Joe. Then turning round again he meant to say, 'Don't let Cosmo catch you, will you?'

But the monster had vanished. Joe was alone again. And his hardest trial was still to come.

Chapter Six
The shining stair

The first thing Joe noticed about the palace was its extreme emptiness. He crept along pale corridors of gleaming marble, ready to bolt if he should meet someone, but he didn't see a sign of life anywhere.

There was emptiness and there was silence. Except that it was not exactly silence because there was the strange, disembodied music, which flowed hauntingly through and around and within everything, like the sea sound in a shell. But there were no human voices, laughing, shouting, whispering. No bustling footsteps. No clattering or clinking. No doors opening and closing.

Where were the maids, gardeners, footmen, butlers and cooks? The important ambassadors? The guards? Though Joe was extremely relieved he didn't run into anyone large and angry, he did begin to wonder after a while if he wasn't being just a little bit *too* lucky.

Supposing the Emperor was watching him all the time without Joe knowing. Supposing he was waiting like a wicked spider for Joe to walk into his magic web. Joe shuddered and it took every scrap of his new courage to keep plodding down the gleaming silent corridors, imagining Cosmo's eyes prickling the back of his neck. But even if he was watched by a thousand invisible spies, Joe knew he had to keep going until he reached the Glass Tower.

'Lady of the Beasts,' he whispered. 'Daughter of All Directions. I promise I'll find you. I really will.' He felt a bit better after he had said her names. As if somehow she had heard him and sent back a sweet silent answer, like the peal of a bell he could only hear *inside*.

All at once he was in Cosmo's banqueting hall. Joe didn't much like the thought of crossing this lavender-scented space with the great polished oak table big enough to dance on, and the carved oak chairs arranged stiffly around it like soldiers. There was nowhere to hide, unless he dived under the table. But it was a beautiful room with a wide window, and when he looked out, Joe could see some distance below him, a familiar figure bounding along the narrow sandy margin of the sea; stopping now and then to look down at its feet in an anxious way, then looking back at the tracks it had made and scratching its fern-frondy head in bewilderment. Joe grinned. He was growing fond of his monster.

Joe leaned against a chair and stood still for a moment, watching him, then he jumped back in alarm as an enormous silver dish came sailing through the air like a spaceship and landed expertly on the table in front of Joe's chair, where it sat, steaming under its lid, filling his nostrils with mouthwatering savoury smells. Seconds later, the dish was followed by a large white china bowl, a silver spoon, a basket containing two white bread rolls and another basket piled with fruit so perfect it was obviously fresh from someone's orchard.

The chair gracefully slid itself a foot or two back from the table, as if inviting Joe to sit down and eat.

Invisible servants, thought Joe amazed. Invisible hands, wafting magically through the air. Was that the secret of Cosmo's empty gleaming palace?

'Thanks all the same,' he said politely to the empty air. 'I'd love to. I'm starving. But this might be Cosmo's supper and I don't think he'd be very pleased if you gave it to me. Perhaps I'll have a bite of anything you've got left over on the way back.'

If I come back, he thought.

The air rippled slightly around him and Joe thought he felt a murmur of disappointment from one of the Invisibles.

'All right,' he said aloud. 'I'll take a roll to keep me going. And some grapes. Thanks.' As he reached out for the bread and fruit the air rippled again, approvingly this time, Joe thought. This was obviously a very motherly Invisible.

With a last regretful look at the steaming dish, wondering if he would ever eat dinner again, he left the enchanted banqueting hall and found himself at the foot of the Shining Stair.

From Skydancer's back, Joe had thought the dizzy stairways of the Palace of Nightfall looked like something in a beautiful dream. Faced with the prospect of climbing one until he reached the Glass Tower, it was more like a terrifying nightmare.

The Shining Stair swooped, soared and

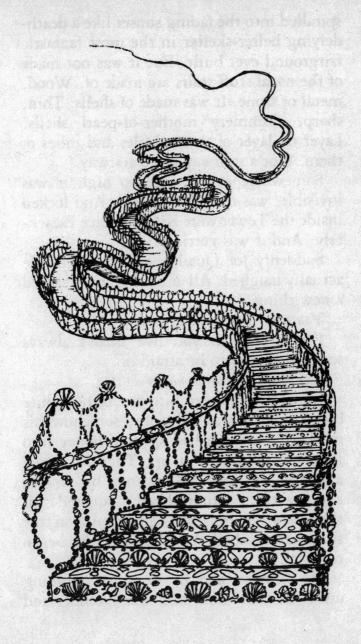

spiralled into the fading sunset like a death-defying helter-skelter in the most fantastic fairground ever built. But it was not made of the usual stuff stairs are made of. Wood, metal or stone. It was made of shells. Thin, sharp, shimmery mother-of-pearl shells. Layer on layer of them. Miles and miles of them. Not a stairway but a starway.

Somewhere at the top, so high it was invisible, was the Glass Tower. And locked inside the Tower were Kit and Alice Fazackerly. And it was getting dark.

Suddenly Joe Quail began to laugh. He actually laughed. All at once he had learned a new thing.

You never stop being afraid.

For as long as you live there's always something new to be afraid of.

But that's no reason not to do it.

Joe took a hungry bite out of his white bread roll. It was delicious; somehow his motherly Invisible had spirited honey into it before he picked it up. Then he tossed a couple of juicy grapes into his mouth and, with a stout heart, squared his shoulders and set his foot firmly on the shimmering shell stairway. And he began to climb.

He climbed and he went on climbing until the air around him was lavender and violet with dusk. He climbed and he went on climbing until the stars came out and the dusk had turned to deep blue darkness all around. He climbed until he could no longer see where he was climbing from or where he was climbing to, until he couldn't see anything at all but the glimmering, starlit stairway under his feet.

He climbed until the magic music had faded away beneath his feet to a far-off sigh. He climbed until his hands and feet were sore from the sharp thin shells. And still he climbed. And a strange thing happened. Joe stopped hating himself. He simply climbed clean out of his old angry self like a worn-out coat and let it flutter away.

He wasn't grumble-guts Joe any more. He wasn't the wrong kind of boy. He was Joe Quail and he was absolutely fine the way he was.

And at the same moment he noticed a star that was larger and brighter than all the others and there was a happy shooting-star *fizz* inside his head and he shouted: 'Star Maiden!' And he knew Alice had told him the third of her many names.

Then the Shining Stairway gave a final dizzying spiral and in front of him was a frail platform, trembling in the wind, and on the platform swayed an even frailer-looking ladder leading straight to the Glass Tower.

But before Joe could even draw breath to shout to Alice and Kit to tell them they were saved at last, a huge and terrifying figure dressed in scarlet and gold, stepped out of the darkness and barred his way.

And what it boomed in its cruel cold voice was this.

'I am the Mighty Cosmo, Emperor of Nightfall and King of Afterdark. And you can't escape me. You're going to die, Joe Quail. I know everything there is to know about you.'

'Oh no you don't,' said Joe, who was so furious at being thwarted so close to the end of his quest that he didn't have much energy left over for being scared.

And then he thought, so I suppose I am going to die, after all. And he felt a terrible choking feeling in his throat and tears came scalding into his eyes. It was such a waste of all he had been through. What was the use of outwitting trolls and defeating dragons? What was the use of climbing the Shining Stair until he climbed right out of his old self, if he was going to allow himself to be beaten now?

Then Joe thought: even if Cosmo is a wicked enchanter, even if he can kill me just by snapping his fingers, I can still put up a fight. He's just a super-big bully, really, and bullies always rely on people being too afraid to fight.

And all the time Joe was thinking, the Mighty Cosmo was waiting at the top of the stairway with a horrible shark-like grin, breathing heavily, getting ready to do whatever terrible thing he was planning to do to Joe.

Later Joe wondered if time had slowed down on the Shining Stairway, because of being so close to the stars. There seemed to be time for far more than the usual number of thoughts to wander through his head. Like, why is it that bullies always smile at you just before they hit you? It was just the same at school when —

And then an astounding idea struck him. It was the combination of the shark-like grin and the heavy breathing. It couldn't be. But it was!

And before he could stop himself he blurted out, 'Hang on, you aren't the Emperor of Nightfall or the King of Afterdark. You liar! You cheat! I know who *you* are. You're just Kevin Kitchener from Number Fifteen. Why aren't you at home in bed?'

There was a gasp like a whale sucking in air before a dive, then the Mighty Cosmo

let out a howl of rage and fear. And, as if
he was only a gold and scarlet fairground
balloon that had been blown up much too
far for its own good, the Emperor deflated.
And as he shrank, so his imperial robes
grew, until they were trailing all along the
platform and down the shell stairway in the
most dangerous and undignified manner.

And Joe Quail wanted to laugh. He
wanted to laugh and laugh until his sides
split like baked apples. He bit his lip fer-
ociously knowing it would be the very worst
thing he could possibly do. It was embar-
rassing enough for Cosmo-Kevin to be
shrunk like a shirt, without being hooted
and guffawed at as well.

But it was such a wonderful joke. However had he blown Kevin up so *huge*? The
way Joe and everyone had run around in
terror of him at school, you'd have thought
Kevin was a second King Kong, towering
over skyscrapers and picking up people in
his gorilla-fists as if they were tiny dolls.

And here he was, just a pale pudgy boy
with a large gold turban sliding gently down
over a pair of dark, unfriendly eyes.

Kevin was either still very shocked or
extremely sulky. Either way he didn't say a
word but only turned a stony white, which
grew whiter and stonier with every passing

second. To his surprise, Joe felt sorry for him and when he was fairly sure he wouldn't shriek with mad laughter as soon as he opened his mouth, he spoke in the most sober and serious voice he could manage.

'Does Alice know who you are?'

Kevin sat down hard on the fragile stair, seeming not to notice the wobble in Joe's voice, or the clouds blowing about under his gigantic, ridiculous curly-toed shoes. He just looked moodily at his knees the way he did at school when Mr Dawlish bellowed at him for forgetting his P.E. kit again.

'No,' he said. 'At least I don't think so. Oh, now you've really gone and spoiled everything. You never should have done what you did, Joe Quail. It's dangerous to have your magic taken away so quickly. You could have killed me, you know. I've got a weak chest.'

Had Joe really taken Kevin's magic away just by calling him by his true name? Just like Rumpelstiltskin, he thought. Only Rumpelstiltskin had stomped his way down through the king's floor in a rage and was never seen again. Joe still had to deal with Kevin.

'You were going to kill me,' he pointed out firmly. 'Or whatever it was you were planning to do with me.'

Time still seemed slowed down and dreamy at the top of the Stairway. Joe had enough time to be amazed all over again at the almost disappointing ordinariness of Kevin Kitchener. However had Kevin managed to swell up so big and bullying in Joe's imagination when in real life he was so short, plump and sulky? In fact, so remarkably like Joe himself. And how was it Joe was suddenly able to see Kevin so clearly since he had come face to face with his own monster under the sea? It was very mysterious, mysterious and magical like everything that had happened to Joe since the moment he met the Afterdark Princess.

Meanwhile Kevin was busily working himself up into a tremendous state of self pity.

'It's horrible at home. No one's ever in and even if they are they never notice me. I pinched some funny glasses off her when she was babysitting those feeble Robinson kids once. They're daft, those Robinsons. They never lock their door. They *deserve* burglars. Anyway, that's how I got here. It's brilliant. I can do just what I like. Everyone's so scared of me I can make them do anything I say.'

'Everyone's scared of you at school, too,' said Joe, remembering.

'Yeah, I make sure of that,' said Kevin with a flash of the old shark-like grin that used to turn Joe's stomach. Then the grin vanished and he was just pale pudgy Kevin Kitchener again. 'But it's dead lonely,' he said. 'If you want to know.'

Joe thought about the many-coloured Palace of Nightfall, rising up from the sea like a magic city and how empty it was and silent except for the strange enchanted music which didn't seem like the sort of sound Kevin would enjoy. And he said: 'It seems quite lonely here to me.'

'Well, you would say that, wouldn't you?' sneered the ex-Emperor of Nightfall, trying to roll up flapping scarlet sleeves so he could find his own pudgy hands and scratch an itch.

Then he said miserably, 'All right. It is. It was fun at first. But it's not any more. And I don't know what to do after I've captured them. Lately I've tried to make friends with them but they just save their dried bread until it's really hard and throw it at me through the bars or call me horrible names.'

Kevin's lip looked as if it was going to wobble.

'I thought you tortured your prisoners,' said Joe, remembering his terrors, 'and things.'

'Only a bit,' said Kevin Kitchener vaguely. 'And I was running out of new ideas.' He brightened. 'Any suggestions?'

'I have got some but not the kind you mean,' said Joe sternly. 'Good ones, though.'

'You mean we could join forces,' said Kevin. 'Two Cosmos. I don't mind. Share the loot. Inspire twice the dread. Shake those Afterdarkers up a bit. That Robin really thinks he's something. Makes me sick with all his swash and buckle. I don't know how his outlaws stood him.'

'No,' said Joe. 'Better than any of that. But before I tell you, you've got to let all the prisoners go. The outlaws and everyone.'

'I was going to do that anyway,' said Kevin.

'And,' said Joe firmly, 'you've got to promise you won't do anything to that poor monster for letting me go. It was getting ill hanging about in the wet and dark. And it was scared out of its mind.'

'No fear,' said Kevin, shaking his head. 'I won't promise that. And you can't make me, either.'

But he looked ashamed.

'Why not?' asked Joe. 'It won't hurt you, you know. It's perfectly tame. I tamed it,' he added modestly. Though he had to admit the monster, once he had finally met him in the light of day, or at least in the light of a match, was never very dreadful.

But Kevin wasn't listening. With his face in his hands he was bawling his eyes out and the only words Joe could understand were, 'I can't. I can't.'

Joe tried patting Kevin awkwardly on his slippery scarlet shoulder but that just made him howl louder. It took a long time for the howls to die down but at last Kevin managed to bellow angrily, 'I can't because if I let him stay free I can't be Emperor any more. And then I won't be anyone. I'll just be Kevin flipping Kitchener for the rest of my life.'

The darkness was lifting, Joe realised. It was nearly morning. He must have been climbing the Shining Stair all through the night.

Out of the darkness the shapes of towers were emerging, with their twirly tops like genies' turbans. Joe thought of the gleaming marble corridors and the banqueting hall where invisible hands produced enchanted feasts out of the air. He thought of the beautiful glowing gardens and fountains and he shivered with sympathy.

He had seen Mr and Mrs Kitchener and he had seen Kevin's big brother and his two big sisters. They all had faces like letter boxes. The tightly closed, sharply biting kind. He understood why Kevin would rather stay here and be waited on by gentle invisible hands.

But Joe knew something else, too. He knew that the Palace of Nightfall didn't belong to Kevin. It had never belonged to the Mighty Cosmo either. Kevin had *stolen* the enchanted palace and the magic that was in it and used it for himself, the same way he had stolen Alice's moonglasses and broken into Afterdark. And he had used all that stolen magic to turn himself into an even bigger bully. That's why everything had gone so wrong. But it didn't have to stay wrong.

Joe began to grin because he thought he saw a way to put things right in both worlds at once. He was pretty sure he knew what Kevin needed because it was what Joe needed, too.

He waited until Kevin reached the hiccupping stage and then he said sternly, 'It won't work, you know. Hiding here, pretending to be wicked, like you do at school. It won't work in the long run. However tall you make yourself, however grand and magical your robes look, you'll always know you're only Kevin Kitchener inside.

Look, Kevin, I didn't like it here at first, but now I think this is the most fantastic world. I want to come again, if I can. But it's no good if you haven't got a —' he drew a deep breath; this was the scary bit.

'If you haven't got a friend.'

There. He'd done it.

Kevin wasn't looking at anything. Just picking the embroidery on his scarlet sleeves. Then, moving on to the embroidery on his golden trousers, he said in a cold voice, 'Are you saying, *you* want to be *my* friend?'

'Well,' said poor Joe, thinking that maybe asking someone to be your friend was far, far worse than trolls, or dragons or the underwater dungeon, or the Shining Stair. 'I know you probably don't — I suppose I shouldn't have —'

Then he felt angry again. Why shouldn't he ask Kevin to be his friend? Yes, why shouldn't he? He was only an ordinary kid, wasn't he? Like Joe?

'Yes,' he said crossly. 'Yes I am. I am asking you to be my friend. Why not? What's wrong with that?'

He narrowed his eyes. He could see something far off, a vague winged shape moving rapidly through the dim light of just before dawn.

'Er – nothing,' said Kevin, and awkwardly he held out a pale and pudgy hand. 'Nothing. There's nothing *wrong*. It's just that no one's ever –'

'I'd like someone to do ordinary things with,' said Joe. 'Someone to go swimming with. And the cinema. And the park. I really like Kit and Maisy. But they've got each other. I know I've got my mum. But she fusses too much and anyway I want someone my own age.'

'I've got a dog,' said Kevin Kitchener not wanting to seem entirely alone in the world. 'His name's Archie. He likes cheese.'

The sun was rising over the edge of the sea and now Joe could see clearly what was speeding towards them through the sky. He began to laugh for the sheer joy and unexpectedness of it.

It was not a flying horse. Not one, not even two or three.

'Stone the crows,' yelled Kevin, suddenly catching sight of them, his mouth falling open. 'It's a whole flipping herd of them!'

Steadily forging through the sunrise, wing deep in raspberry-ripple cloud they came, one after another, seven winged horses; their manes flying, their eyes shining, their breath streaming out in silver clouds. Skydancer had returned with reinforcements.

And at the same moment Joe, remembering, felt in his pocket and fished out what the monster had given him. It was not a pebble and it wasn't quite a shell. It was a key, a perfect key made out of shining, rainbow-coloured shell stuff. The key to the door of the Glass Tower. Joe's quest was over.

'It's all right,' he called to the seven flying horses who were now purposefully circling the tower where Alice and Kit were still imprisoned. 'It's all right. I've got the key, look! We've just got to let them out and make sure the monster is all right, then we can all go home, if you'll take us –'

The next part took no time.

'So there you are, Joe,' said Alice cheerfully, when he opened the door. 'I knew you'd come. I told you there was more to you than meets the eye, Joe Quail. But we'd better hurry. I don't know if I told you but we always have to get back by sunrise.'

Joe stood and looked at Alice, the last Princess of Afterdark. She was as fresh as a daisy, perfectly at home on the shimmering sea-shell stairway with clouds blowing around her feet. She was at home wherever she was, he thought.

Didn't anything surprise her? Had she always known that Kevin was the false Emperor who had stolen the palace away from the true ruler of Nightfall? Had she known all the time that Joe wasn't the wrong kind of boy but only needed the right kind of adventure to sort him out?

There were so many questions he wanted to ask but there wasn't time. The sun was lifting itself over the rim of the sea, lion-haired and flaming, and they had to go home.

'Hallo,' said Kit, coming out, rubbing his eyes. 'Hey, what's Kevin Kitchener doing here?'

'I'll explain later,' said Joe. 'Skydancer has brought some friends to take us home. But what about Maisy?' he remembered.

'Robin will get her back,' said Alice, who seemed to know everything that had happened without needing to be told and she vaulted lightly on to the back of a fiery red and golden mare, grabbing the mane of a blue-silvery mount for Kit. But Joe only wanted to ride one horse home; sensible, ivory, faintly green-marbled all over. The most unlikely flying horse in the world.

Joe made Skydancer circle in low before he let him fly away from the palace.

And there on the seaweedy margin of wet sand, as Joe had known he would be, was the monster thoughtfully studying its own footprints. It had made elaborate trails, weaving in and out in a wild, dancing, changing pattern. Birdprints. Webbed feet. Prints that might be lion or bear. And the latest ones that looked almost like the prints a child might make, running barefoot across the shore towards the sea.

'Hallo,' called the monster, waving to Joe and pointing to a pair of small flamingo pink and green, almost human feet. 'I've nearly got them right now.'

It was still changing, Joe thought. He got the oddest feeling that when he came back next time the monster might have changed itself into something else entirely. It seemed to be trying out different shapes. An experimental gauzy trembling around its shoulders suggested it might even break out in a stubby rainbow wing or two just for the fun of it.

This, Joe realised, was and always had been the true Master of Nightfall, this was the shy genie who had built the fantastic impossible palace, filling it with sea-shell music and kindly invisible hands; a gentle, childlike enchanter who, once he had recovered from his long imprisonment, would rule his country as playfully and wisely as it deserved.

'Goodbye, oh goodbye, dear, dear monster,' Joe called out as Skydancer carried him away.

'Afterdark is safe now,' he said to himself. 'Afterdark and Nightfall will always be friends from now on.'

Then he yawned hugely and there was a blur of sunrise into cloudscape; the sound of waves dissolving into the sound of wind rushing in the forest or perhaps the sound of wings beating. Then doors opening and closing and a gentle settling into something soft.

'He fell asleep so quickly,' a calm sensible voice was saying, 'he never needed the cough mixture, Mrs Quail.'

'Don't shut the cupboard door any more, Mum,' murmured Joe. 'It really hates to be shut in.'

But he was only talking in his sleep, smiling, his hair drifting back gently from his face so that his mother thought it looked almost as if he were flying through the air.

Chapter Seven
Turning the wind

'Kevin,' said Joe when school was over. 'Can I bring Kit and Maisy over to see you after tea?'

'No thanks,' said Kevin gruffly. 'If your mum doesn't mind I'd rather come round to your house.'

'Can you bring Archie?' said Joe hopefully. 'We've got plenty of cheese.'

'All right,' said Kevin. 'See you.'

'See you, Joe, see you, Kevin,' yelled Kit and Maisy tearing past in a multi-coloured blur like a two-headed hurricane.

'Sorry I'm so late,' said Joe's mum, arriving out of breath at the school gate. 'Have you had a nice day?' She beamed in a tired way at Kit and Maisy and gave a worried look at Kevin loping off alone in the direction of home. 'Was that dreadful boy bullying you again?'

'Kevin?' said Joe in amazement, as if he'd never heard of such a thing. 'Let him try. No, he's coming round later with Kit and Maisy.' Then he said excitedly, 'Just a minute, Mum, I want to ask Alice something.' He had spotted a familiar figure wheeling a bicycle along the road. She was talking to a ragged old man, his collar turned up against the bitter wind.

He raced off through the crowd of Golden Street Juniors' children, his shirt flying, one sock falling down, calling, 'Alice, Alice! Wait for me.'

By the time he had dodged in and out to reach her the old man was nowhere to be seen, but Alice stopped at once and turned to him, her shining brown rope of hair swinging over her shoulder, her grey eyes friendly.

'Hallo, Joe,' she said. 'I hope you didn't have any bad dreams last night? No trolls or dragons or terrible monsters?' She was teasing, he saw. He grinned back, wondering if somewhere amongst her homework books there really was a book called *The*

Observer Book of Monsters. He badly wanted to read that book one day.

He gazed at Alice, drinking her in. How had he ever believed she was dull and ordinary? If he dared to gaze into her eyes now, right here in the middle of the street, would he find himself falling through moonlight, running through the forest in the shape of a fawn?

'Aren't you going to speak to me too, Joe?' said another voice. 'Or don't you recognise me any more?'

'Robin,' said Joe, startled. And of course he should have known this tall, lion-haired boy, carrying Alice's sensible school-bag over his shoulder, and he grinned back at once, feeling the familiar golden sunburst in his chest.

For a long while Joe stood looking from one to the other, quite unable to speak. There are some things that simply can't be put into words.

'Joe,' his mother was calling. 'Time to go home, Joe.'

Shyly he said, 'I've got to go now. Well – see you.' And he began to turn away.

'Wait,' said Alice. 'You forgot something last night.' She fished something out of her bike basket. ''Bye, Joe Quail. Be seeing you soon, I expect.'

But Joe hardly glanced at what she gave him. He was staring after them, rooted to the spot. He wasn't staring at Alice or Robin. He was staring at Alice's sensible bottle-green bicycle.

It couldn't be. It just couldn't be. The painted name was worn, the gold lettering almost rubbed away. SKYDAN. Anyway it was impossible. A bike was a bike.

The way sensible Alice Fazackerly was a wild outlaw princess with pistols in her belt?

The way Zoom the stripy cat was a tiger?

The way Forest Street –

Perhaps in Afterdark it *was* possible, thought Joe. Once you put on moonglasses,

there is more to everything than meets the eye.

For the first time he looked properly at the stiff, rolled-up piece of paper Alice had given him and, feverishly unrolling it, realised what he was holding. The map of his quest to the Palace of Nightfall.

But at the top in Coll's old-fashioned loopy script was written something new.

Joe's First Adventure in Afterdark.

'So there will be other adventures,' he whispered to himself. 'I knew there would. I just *knew* there would.'

And, leaping high into the air he shouted for the sheer wild noise of it, and began to race back to his mother; a boy who could run and climb and swim; a boy who wasn't afraid of monsters or magicians. A boy made for danger as fishes swim in the sea.

So that seeing him hurtle towards her, his face glowing, his mother thought: good heavens, what *does* Alice do to them? He's a changed child.

Then Joe stopped dead in his headlong dash and he did the strangest thing.

He licked his finger and held it up in the bitter easterly wind and said quietly: 'Turn!'

And all the leaves and sweetpapers and little stinging flying piles of dust that had been blowing in one direction, danced a little on the spot and then they began to blow *backwards*.

Then as Joe came racing up, catching hold of both her hands, laughing, delighted with himself, shouting, 'Did you see that — I turned the wind! I really turned the wind!' for a moment, just for a moment, Joe's mum thought she caught a wonderful, slightly familiar, fragrance of rosemary and violets.

Of course she knew Joe was just pretending. She knew such things just weren't possible, but suddenly she felt so unexpectedly happy that she began to run along too, pulling Joe with her.

'I'll race you,' she shouted. 'I'll race you home. Last one past the gate has to put the kettle on.'

Alice Fazackerly watched the gleeful flying figures growing smaller and smaller until they vanished altogether at the end of Golden Street. Then she smiled, a strange sweet smile and her grey eyes were bright as though she was entirely satisfied with what she had seen.

'All the same,' she murmured, 'that's quite enough of that for now.' And holding up one finger she gently turned the wind back again.

'Hey! Crazy weather, isn't it!' called a red-haired girl, struggling past on her bike.

'Can't make up its mind. Want to come round to my house tonight, Alice?'

'Oh, I'd love to, Debbie,' said Alice Fazackerly regretfully. 'But I'm afraid I can't – I've promised to babysit again tonight.'